## DATE DUE

| | |
|---|---|
| | APR 0 9 |
| JAN 2 8 | APR ~~DISCARDED~~ |
| FEB 1 0 | MAY 0 5 |
| FEB 1 1 | |
| | MAY 1 4 |
| FEB 1 8 | |
| MAR 0 4 | |
| MAR 1 7 | |
| MAR 2 5  APR 0 9 | |

Jr. Graphic Mysteries™

# GHOSTS IN AMITYVILLE

## The Haunted House

Jack DeMolay

**PowerKiDS**
press

New York

Published in 2007 by The Rosen Publishing Group, Inc.
29 East 21st Street, New York, NY 10010

First Edition

Editors: Melissa Acevedo and Joanne Randolph
Book Design: Ginny Chu
Illustrations: Q2A

Library of Congress Cataloging-in-Publication Data

DeMolay, Jack.
  Ghosts in Amityville : the haunted house / by Jack DeMolay.— 1st ed.
      p. cm. — (Jr. graphic mysteries)
  Includes index.
   ISBN (10) 1-4042-3402-0 — (13) 978-1-4042-3402-4 (library binding) — ISBN
(10) 1-4042-2155-7 — (13) 978-1-4042-2155-0 (pbk)
   1.  Ghosts—New York (State)—Amityville—Juvenile literature. 2.  Haunted houses—New
York (State)—Amityville—Juvenile literature.  I. Title. II. Series.

BF1472.U6 M385 2007
133.1'2974725—dc22

                                                                        2006001590

Manufactured in the United States of America

# Contents

# GHOSTS IN AMITYVILLE: THE HAUNTED HOUSE

IT ALL BEGAN ON A CHILLY DECEMBER DAY IN 1975, WHEN THE LUTZ FAMILY MOVED INTO THEIR NEW HOME ON OCEAN AVENUE IN AMITYVILLE, NEW YORK.

THEIR TIME THERE WOULD BEGIN ONE OF THE MOST FAMOUS GHOST STORIES IN AMERICA.

THE TRUTH OF THE STORY HAS LONG BEEN **DEBATED**, BUT PEOPLE REMAIN INTERESTED IN THE STORY TO THIS DAY.

THE HOUSE WAS A DREAM COME TRUE FOR THE LUTZES AND THEIR THREE YOUNG CHILDREN.

I CAN'T BELIEVE IT'S OURS, GEORGE.

THIS WAS A HAPPY DAY.

DANNY! LET'S CHECK OUT THE BOATHOUSE!

EVEN SO THE LUTZES THOUGHT ABOUT THE **HORRORS** THAT TOOK PLACE IN THE HOUSE ONE YEAR EARLIER.

ONE YEAR AGO, A HORRIBLE CRIME HAD SHOCKED THE PEACEFUL SEASIDE TOWN OF AMITYVILLE.

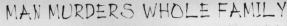

MAN MURDERS WHOLE FAMILY

OH MY! NO ONE'S LEFT ALIVE!

COME QUICK! WE FOUND THE KILLER!

RONALD DEFEO JR. HAD KILLED HIS PARENTS, BROTHERS, AND SISTERS.

DEFEO SAID THAT VOICES HAD TOLD HIM WHAT TO DO.

DEFEO WAS FOUND **GUILTY**. NOW HE WAS SERVING THE REST OF HIS LIFE IN JAIL.

BEFORE THEY MOVED IN, GEORGE AND KATHY LUTZ HAD LEARNED THE **FRIGHTENING** HISTORY OF THEIR HOUSE.

GEORGE, ARE YOU THINKING ABOUT THE MURDERS, TOO?

THE SHOCKING STORY WAS NOT GOING TO STOP THEM FROM OWNING THE HOUSE OF THEIR DREAMS.

EVERYTHING WILL BE FINE. THE HOUSE IS OURS NOW.

THE LUTZES BEGAN TO SETTLE INTO THEIR NEW LIFE.

HOWEVER, UNUSUAL EVENTS OCCURRED FROM ALMOST THE MOMENT THEY ARRIVED.

EXCUSE ME, GEORGE?

I AM GLAD YOU COULD COME!

GEORGE HAD ASKED A **PARANORMAL EXPERT** TO CHECK THE HOUSE BECAUSE OF THE VOICES DEFEO SAID HE HAD HEARD.

WHILE HE WAS CHECKING THE HOUSE, THE PARANORMAL EXPERT FELT SOMETHING STRANGE.

WILL YOU USE THAT CORNER ROOM AS A BEDROOM?

NO, WE ARE GOING TO USE IT AS A SEWING ROOM. WHY?

THERE WAS JUST SOMETHING THERE THAT MADE ME FEEL UNCOMFORTABLE.

GEORGE WONDERED IF WHATEVER THE EXPERT HAD FELT WAS CONNECTED TO THE EVILS THAT HAD TAKEN PLACE IN HIS NEW HOME.

DADDY! DADDY!

HARRY'S STUCK! HE'S CHOKING!

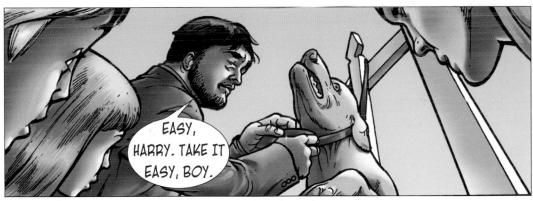

EASY, HARRY. TAKE IT EASY, BOY.

HARRY LIVED BUT THE TROUBLE WAS JUST BEGINNING FOR THE LUTZES.

HE'S OKAY!

STRANGE THINGS STARTED TO HAPPEN TO THE LUTZES.

TERRIBLE SMELLS BEGAN TO FILL THE HOUSE.

AGAIN? IT'S WINTER!

LARGE NUMBERS OF FLIES WERE OFTEN FOUND IN THE SEWING ROOM.

A BLACK LIQUID **OOZED** FROM THE KEYHOLES IN DOORS AND FROM AIR **VENTS**.

HOWEVER, THE HOUSE WAS NOT THE ONLY THING ACTING STRANGELY.

GEORGE WOULD SUDDENLY WAKE UP DURING THE NIGHT.

HE FELT A STRANGE NEED TO CHECK ON THINGS IN THE BOATHOUSE.

KATHY HAD **NIGHTMARES** ALL THE TIME.

GEORGE WAS OFTEN VERY SICK.

THERE WAS ALSO A LOT OF FIGHTING.

THE FAMILY STARTED TO HEAR STRANGE NOISES.

BOOM BOOM

THERE'S SOMEONE IN THE ATTIC!

WE'RE COMING, SON!

GEORGE! THAT SOUNDED LIKE THE FRONT DOOR!

SLAM

THE LUTZES HEARD THOSE NOISES EVERY NIGHT. GEORGE WOULD RUSH TO FIND WHERE THEY WERE COMING FROM.

I DON'T UNDERSTAND. THIS IS THE ONLY DOOR THAT MAKES THAT SOUND.

GEORGE WOULD THEN GO BACK UPSTAIRS.

SOON HE WOULD HEAR NEW SOUNDS COMING FROM THE FIRST FLOOR.

WHO'S THERE? WHO IS IT?!

WHEN HE REACHED THE LIVING ROOM HE FOUND THAT THE FURNITURE HAD BEEN MOVED.

THEY DECIDED NOT TO LET THE HOUSE SCARE THEM.

THE LUTZES DECIDED TO HAVE A DINNER PARTY FOR THEIR NEIGHBORS.

HERE'S TO YOUR NEW HOME, FOLKS!

WHAT WAS THAT?

BOOM BOOM BOOM

YOU HEAR THAT, TOO?

THEY ALL LISTENED FROM THE STAIRS. THEY WONDERED WHERE THE NOISE CAME FROM.

DO YOU THINK IT WAS THE GHOSTS OF THE DEFEO FAMILY?

THE LUTZES AND THEIR GUESTS WENT FROM ROOM TO ROOM TRYING TO FIND THE SOURCE OF THE NOISES.

THEY EVEN TRIED BEGGING ANY SPIRITS WHO MIGHT BE HAUNTING THE HOUSE TO STOP.

BOOM BOOM BOOM

NOTHING WORKED.

WHEN THEIR GUESTS LEFT, THE LUTZES WERE ONCE AGAIN ALONE IN THEIR HAUNTED HOUSE.

ODD THINGS OFTEN HAPPENED WHEN KATHY WAS IN THE KITCHEN.

SHE WOULD OFTEN FEEL A **PRESENCE** BEHIND HER.

THE FAMILY ALSO SAW GLOWING EYES LOOKING IN THE WINDOWS.

SHADOWS FILLED THE HOUSE.

DO SHADOWS TALK?

MISSY ANNOUNCED THAT SHE HAD MADE AN **IMAGINARY** FRIEND.

JODIE SAYS HE'S SCARED OF THE WIND.

WHO IS JODIE, HONEY?

JODIE'S MY FRIEND. HE CAN CHANGE HIS SHAPE.

HE SAYS HE LIKES THIS HOUSE.

HE SAYS I AM GOING TO LIVE HERE FOREVER.

THE LUTZES WERE SHOCKED.

THE HORRORS CONTINUED.

THERE ARE THOSE EYES AGAIN, GEORGE!

LEAVE US ALONE! DO YOU HEAR ME?

GEORGE RAN OUTSIDE AND MADE A STRANGE **DISCOVERY**.

ARE THOSE HOOFPRINTS?

THESE HORRIBLE EVENTS WERE DRIVING THE FAMILY MAD.

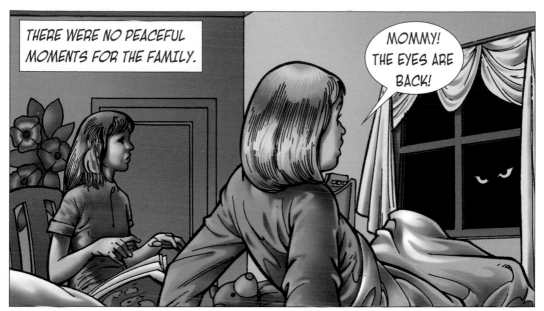

THERE WERE NO PEACEFUL MOMENTS FOR THE FAMILY.

MOMMY! THE EYES ARE BACK!

THE FAMILY FOUGHT BACK.

CRASH

THE HOUSE DID NOT LIKE THAT AT ALL.

SQUEAL

I CAN'T TAKE THIS ANYMORE.

THE HOUSE HAD WON.

THE LUTZES RUSHED TO LEAVE THE HOUSE.

THE WALLS OF THE HOUSE SEEMED TO MOVE AROUND. THEY HEARD GROANING NOISES.

RUN!

AS GEORGE TRIED TO LEAVE, HE MET A GHOST. HE HOPED IT WAS THE LAST ONE HE WOULD EVER SEE.

RUN! RUN!

DAYS LATER PARANORMAL **INVESTIGATORS** CAME TO THE HOUSE.

IT LOOKS LIKE THESE FOLKS LEFT IN A HURRY. SOMETHING IN THIS HOUSE SCARED THEM.

THE INVESTIGATORS CHECKED ALL OF THE ROOMS IN THE HOUSE.

THERE IS DEFINITELY A HORRIBLE PRESENCE IN THIS HOME.

I HOPE I NEVER FEEL SOMETHING LIKE THAT AGAIN!

MANY YEARS HAVE PASSED, BUT THE LUTZES CONTINUE TO STICK TO THEIR STORY OF THE HORRORS THEY **ENDURED** DURING THEIR ONE MONTH STAY IN AMITYVILLE.

THE END

# Did You Know?

- Many people who have studied the Amityville story believe it is just a hoax, or joke. Some people believe it was a way for the Lutz family to get attention and make money.

- Some people believe a witch named John Ketcham once owned the house in Amityville.

- Two movies have been made about the house in Amityville. Both movies were filmed in Toms River, New Jersey, not Amityville, New York.

- No one living in the house at 112 Ocean Avenue has reported any ghostly activity since the Lutz family did.

- Before they bought the house in Amityville, the Lutzes looked at over 50 houses to buy. They paid $80,000 for the house.

# Glossary

**debated** (dih-BAYT-ed)  Argued.

**discovery** (dis-KUH-vuh-ree)  Something that has been found for the first time.

**endured** (en-DURD)  Suffered.

**expert** (EK-spert)  A person who knows a lot about a subject.

**frightening** (FRY-ten-ing)  Scary.

**guilty** (GIl-tee)  Having done something wrong or against the law.

**horrors** (HOHR-uhrz)  Things that cause great shock or harm.

**imaginary** (ih-MAH-juh-ner-ee)  Made up.

**investigators** (in-VES tuh-guy-terz)  People who try to learn the facts about something.

**nightmares** (NYT-mehrz)  Scary dreams.

**oozed** (OOZD)  Passed or flowed slowly through a small opening.

**paranormal** (pa-ruh-NOR-mul)  Not able to be explained by science.

**presence** (PREH-zens)  Something felt or believed to be present.

**vents** (VENTS)  Openings that let air or liquid in or out.

# Index

**B**
black liquid, 10
boathouse, 5, 11

**D**
Defeo, Ronald, Jr., 6, 8
dinner party, 14

**G**
ghost(s), 15, 20
glowing eyes, 16

**H**
hoofprints, 18

**L**
Lutz, George, 5, 7–9, 11–13,
    18, 20
Lutz, Kathy, 7, 11, 16
Lutz, Missy, 17

**N**
nightmares, 11

**P**
paranormal expert, 8
paranormal investigators, 21

**S**
sewing room, 8, 10
shadows, 16

# Web Sites

Due to the changing nature of Internet links, the Rosen Publishing Group, Inc., has developed an online list of Web sites related to the subject of this book. This site is updated regularly. Please use this link to access the list:
www.powerkidslinks.com/jgm/amityvil/